P9-BBO-264

Home to Medicine Mountain

Written by CHIORI SANTIAGO   Illustrated by JUDITH LOWRY

CHILDREN'S BOOK PRESS, an imprint of LEE & LOW BOOKS INC.
New York

BENNY LEN AND STANLEY'S JOURNEY

YO-TIM YAMNE
(MEDICINE MOUNTAIN)

WESTWOOD

SUSANVILLE

MARYSVILLE

SACRAMENTO

CALIFORNIA

FRESNO

BARSTOW

SAN BERNADINO

RIVERSIDE

*T*his book is based on a true story.

My people have lived in the mountains of northern California for many centuries. They belong to the Mountain Maidu and the Hamawi Pit-River tribes. In the old days, they hunted deer and gathered roots, vegetables and acorns in the beautiful baskets they made. Everything they needed to make a good life was around them.

The lives of my people changed in many ways after the European settlers came. One change was that Indian children were taken to boarding schools to live apart from their families for the entire school year. These schools were created especially for Indian children with the idea that they needed to unlearn their Indian ways and live as the settlers did.

My grandparents went to these schools and so did their children, including my uncle Stanley and my dad, who was called "Benny Len." Their school in Riverside was hundreds of miles from their home in Susanville near Yo-Tim Yamne (Medicine Mountain). Although the school paid for children to take the train to get there, it did not always pay to send them home for summer vacation. This is the story of how my dad and uncle found their way home one summer in the 1930s, when they were very young.

—Judith Lowry

BENNY LEN STARED OUT the window. He listened to the train's wheels singing a sad song, mile after mile, carrying him and Stanley away from home. For two days, the wheels beat a rhythm as they left the pine woods of Medicine Mountain to roll through small towns, golden hills, then desert dotted with boulders and sage brush.

At last, the train stopped in a place as flat and hot as a giant's griddle. The children felt restless and cranky, bad as an itch that needs scratching. Stanley and another boy wrestled in the dirt. Benny Len stood with the others, waiting.

A man and woman came to take them to the boarding school. With them came two students in school uniforms. Benny Len couldn't help staring at their feet. They were wearing hard, stiff leather shoes. Benny Len, like the other children from the train, was barefoot. He tried to imagine wearing shoes all the time. He curled his toes into the dirt to remind himself how the earth felt, comforting under his feet.

At the school, Benny Len and Stanley were given uniforms and stiff, new shoes. Benny Len's feet no longer touched the earth. His uniform was scratchy, not soft like his old overalls. He no longer heard the sounds of Susanville—the music of birds in the pines and wind in the branches. The boarding school was a world of sharp edges, shiny surfaces and shouting bells.

Every morning at six o'clock, the children pulled on their uniforms and marched from their dormitories to the grassy yard. Before, they were Indian children from everywhere, speaking their own languages, wearing clothes their grandmothers made. Now, in their uniforms, they looked all the same, like a row of birds on a fence.

"Forward march! Left face!" Teacher's voice rang as the children practiced marching in close order drill up and down the yard. Back home, people danced in circles to honor the earth. "Here," Benny Len thought, "they march in squares." He lifted his feet high and made a nice sharp turn when the line turned left.

In the dining hall, Benny Len looked at his bowl of cereal and felt homesick. He thought of the flapjack and bean sandwiches his grandma made for breakfast. He could almost taste them.

"Hurry up and eat that stuff," said Stanley. "We only have fifteen minutes!"

In every classroom, the round eye of a clock stared from the wall, measuring time in neat little lines. Benny Len watched Teacher writing lines of words on the blackboard. They reminded him of an army of ants marching in close order drill.

Benny Len and Stanley spoke English at home, but other children had to remember not to use their Indian languages in school. Once, in class, Benny Len heard two Navajo girls in front of him whispering together.

"Speak English!" he warned. "If Teacher hears you, you'll get it!"

"No talking, young man." Benny Len looked up to see Teacher standing next to him. She held a ruler in one hand.

"Yes, ma'am," Benny Len nodded. He studied the blackboard. He wished Teacher would tell them their lessons in stories, as his grandmother did. If she were here, she would tell him about the Moon, who stole the grandchild of Old Frog Woman, and how Old Frog Woman went to rescue the boy from Moon's ice-covered house.

"Leonard! Are you daydreaming again?" Teacher sighed. "You would be an excellent student, Leonard, if you just paid attention. No softball for you today. You may sweep the dining room instead, and think about why you're being punished."

1492 Discovery of America
Manifest destiny
Louisiana Purchase
1849 Gold rush of California

At night the children slept in their dormitories, one child in each bed, each bed in a long row. Benny Len felt lonely by himself under the blanket. At home, he and Stanley and their cousins piled into one bed, laughing and joking and fighting over the covers.

"Lights out," said the matron. "Quiet, now."

Every night in the dark, Benny Len listened to the clock. It ticked away the time, always the same amount of time between each tick. Benny Len lay on his back and stared at the long, blank ceiling. He turned on his side and looked at the rows of iron cots, each with a green army blanket on top of a sleeping child. He couldn't sleep.

Not far away, he heard one of the little boys crying, making soft sounds like a boiling pot of acorn soup.

"Shush. You're going to be OK." Benny Len heard Stanley's voice in the dark. Bit by bit, as Stanley whispered, the other little boy stopped crying and fell asleep. Benny Len felt better, too, knowing Stanley wasn't far away.

He fell asleep dreaming of home.

In his dream, Benny Len was at his grandmother's house.
It was a cold night in winter, and he and Grandmother were
snug in one bed. She was telling Benny Len about Pa'nom, the
brave brown bear that watches over the people who live near
Medicine Mountain.

"We are the people of the bear," she said. "If you really need
help, the bear will protect you. Remember that if you are ever
far away, my little cub."

Dreams let Benny Len travel home whenever he wanted. In his dreams, he lived once again in Grandmother's house during the long days of summer. While she gathered healing herbs on Medicine Mountain, he chopped wood for the cooking fire. He carried heavy pails of water from the spring. He stood at the window to thread the long, silver needles his grandmother used for beadwork. He liked to watch her fingers moving quickly, like the flames in the iron stove.

Time was different at Grandmother's house. It didn't march in neat rows. Some days were slow as a waterbug drifting downstream in summer. Others slipped by as quickly as a coyote melting into the shadows.

Sometimes, when the stars came out, they walked to the roundhouse to watch the men sing and dance around the fire in their feather capes. As they walked, his grandmother's hand wrapped around his.

"You're almost a man, little cub," she would say, smiling down at Benny Len.

His dreams took him to the bear dance, which happens each year when the bears wake from their winter sleep. He heard men playing clap sticks. Leaves of sweet-smelling *munmuni* decorated their ears. He saw his family around the dance circle with their necklaces of *munmuni* leaves. A big brown bear danced in the circle.

His uncle held the *yo'koli* flag, its tassels of maple bark waving gently. Beneath the flag, the bear danced toward Benny Len and Stanley. The boys weren't scared. They knew the animal was really their friend, Seymour Smith, dressed in a bearskin, dancing like the spirit of the bear.

Months went by at the boarding school. Benny Len learned to read and to add long rows of numbers. He played on the softball team with his pals, Tommy Jackson and Woody Napa. He worked hard, and he stayed out of trouble.

One day, when he and Stanley were raking the yard, Benny Len saw Woody walking to the train stop with a group of friends. Woody waved. He and the other boys were going home for the summer.

"Will we go home soon?" Benny Len asked his brother.

"We're not going home," Stanley said. He leaned on his rake. "The school only pays for the ticket to come here, not to go home. We'll stay and work around the school. We'll go home next year."

Benny Len didn't want to hear Stanley's words. He felt tears pressing against his eyelids. He blinked quickly so the tears wouldn't squeeze out.

He felt Stanley looking at him.

"You really want to go, don't you?" Stanley asked.

Benny Len thought that if he said anything, he would cry, so he just nodded.

Stanley looked at him a long time. Finally he said, "Don't worry. I'll think of a way to get us home."

Late that night, Benny Len dreamed of the bear dance. In the middle of the dance, the big brown bear reached out, grabbed Benny Len by the shoulder and shook him.

Benny Len laughed. The bear shook harder. Benny Len opened his eyes. There was no bear.

It was Stanley, trying to wake him up.

"Shhhh. Quiet," Stanley whispered. The room was dark. Everyone was asleep. Through the windows, silver light from the full moon washed over the rows of beds.

"Quick, get your stuff," said Stanley. "I figured out a way to go home. But we have to get out of here right now."

Stanley took the blanket off Benny Len's bed and rolled it up with some of Benny Len's extra clothes inside. Benny Len saw that Stanley had a blanket roll, too. Barefoot, they tiptoed to the hall. No one was there. As quickly and quietly as deer, they slipped from the dark box of the building and ran across the yard in the moonlight.

"We're going to ride the rails," Stanley explained when they stopped in the shadows. "That's what people do when they don't have money for a ticket. I've seen them."

Stanley looked down at his little brother. "Now, you have to listen well. When I say GO, follow me as fast as you can."

Benny Len nodded.

"We're going to climb a ladder all the way to the top of the boxcar. Think you can do that?"

"Sure," Benny Len said. At home, he could shimmy up a tree by the time Stanley counted to ten. "A ladder's easy," he said.

"Good. You're not scared, now, are you?" Stanley asked.

"No." Benny Len shook his head. Even though he was scared, a little.

The moon looked down as the boys ran toward the midnight train. Benny Len's heart pounded like a hundred clap sticks in his ears. They waited until the watchman passed by, then, one behind the other, they climbed the ladder to the top of a boxcar. Benny Len gripped the ladder with his bare toes. His feet felt free without the heavy leather shoes.

They were safe on top of the boxcar. The sky spread a starry blanket over them. Stanley took a piece of rope, wrapped it around Benny Len and tied it around the railing on the top of the train.

"There," Stanley said. "Now you can go to sleep, and you won't fall off."

The train began to move, creaking and groaning. The wind pushed against their faces. Stanley put one arm around his brother's shoulders as the train moved faster and faster. Benny Len yawned. After he fell asleep, Stanley stayed awake a long time, watching the stars.

They rode back through the desert, past golden hills hunched like hunters waiting for deer, past flat green fields, farmhouses and towns. One night they rolled into a train yard, where they climbed onto another train heading north. In the day, Benny Len looked at all of Earthmaker's land rolling by and listened to the train wheels singing his name: Benny Len, Benny Len, Benny Len. He felt so free that he raised his arms to the sky. He felt as if he were flying.

Early in the morning, Stanley woke Benny Len.

"Look!" he said. Ahead, the peak of Medicine Mountain rose tall and proud. Benny Len's heart smiled. He knew that just a little farther, their town lay waiting in the valley between the mountains.

"I told you I'd get us home," said Stanley.

As the train rumbled into Susanville, its whistle sounded like a great long laugh. When no one was looking, the boys climbed down the side of the boxcar and ran all the way home.

Even from far away, Benny Len and Stanley could see their father sitting on the steps of their house. As they got near, they saw their sisters, who were too little to go to school, playing in front. Juanita, the oldest, ran towards them, laughing.

"Mama! Grandmother!" Stanley shouted. Their mother was hanging out the wash. She was so surprised to see them, she stood as still as an oak tree. Grandmother sat nearby, holding their baby sister Virginia in her cradleboard. She watched them run toward her, smiling for her brave bear cubs.

That night, Stanley and Benny Len filled themselves with their mother's good food and the sound of their family's laughter. They listened once again to their grandmother's stories of cleverness and courage.

Now Benny Len and Stanley had their own story. They'd ridden the rails and seen miles of land between the place where day breaks and the place where the sun goes down. The lessons they learned from the journey would be with them always.

For the rest of the summer, and for many years after, Benny Len and Stanley told the story of their adventure on the train. They told it to their children and their grandchildren. Always, one of the children would ask: "Did you have to go back to the boarding school?"

"Yes," Benny Len or Stanley would answer, remembering.

They didn't mind the long journey so much after that. They were sure they would be back for the bear dance every year, because now they knew the way home.

Home to Medicine Mountain *is the story of how artist Judith Lowry's father and uncle found their way home from an Indian boarding school in the 1930s. Her father, Leonard (right), and her uncle, Stanley (left), both had distinguished careers in the U.S. armed forces. Now retired, they live close to each other in Susanville, California.*

Judith Lowry, *of Mountain Maidu, Hamawi Pit-River, and Australian descent, is considered one of California's premiere contemporary Native American artists. She spent most of her early life living in many different parts of the world when her father was a career army officer. She feels that the experience of growing up mixed race against the backdrop of different cultural settings has provided her with an interesting worldview from which she draws much of her artistic inspiration. She is also greatly inspired by the stories passed down in her family. Judith lives in Nevada City, California.*

Chiori Santiago *writes for national magazines about the art, music, and family life of people from many parts of the world. As a child, she and her family lived in Asia and Europe when her father worked with the Asia Foundation. Of Japanese, Italian, and Native American descent, Chiori believes that being mixed race and having lived in various cultures has greatly influenced her perspective as a writer. She feels that the common childhood experiences she and Judith shared gave her the personal insight and connection she needed for this project. Chiori lives in Berkeley, California.*

Story copyright © 1998 by Chiori Santiago
Pictures copyright © 1998 by Judith Lowry
All rights reserved. No part of this book may be reproduced, transmitted, or stored in an information retrieval system in any form or by any means, electronic, mechanical, photocopying, recording, or otherwise, without written permission from the publisher.
Children's Book Press, an imprint of LEE & LOW BOOKS Inc., 95 Madison Avenue, New York, NY 10016
leeandlow.com

Book design: Katherine Tillotson
Book production: The Kids at Our House
Book editor: Harriet Rohmer

Thanks to the LEF Foundation for their contribution toward the publication of this book. Thanks to Malcolm Margolin, David Schecter, and Janeen Antoine.
For additional resources on California Indians contact:
Heyday Books, P.O. Box 9145, Berkeley, CA 94709, heydaybooks.com

Library of Congress Cataloging-in-Publication Data
Santiago, Chiori.
Home to Medicine Mountain / written by Chiori Santiago ;
illustrated by Judith Lowry.   p.   cm.
Summary: Two young Maidu Indian brothers sent to live at a government-run Indian residential school in California in the 1930s find a way to escape and return home for the summer.
ISBN 978-0-89239-176-9 (paperback)
1. Maidu Indians—Juvenile fiction.
[1. Maidu Indians—Fiction. 2. Boarding schools—Fiction. 3. Indians of North America—California—Fiction.] I. Lowry, Judith, ill. II. Title.
E99.M18L68   1998   [Fic]—dc21   97-52987   CIP   AC
Manufactured in China by Jade Productions
15   14   13   12   11   10   9
First Edition